The PEAR TREE

A folktale retold by Luli Gray
Illustrated by Madelyn Goodnight

Penny Candy Books
Oklahoma City & Savannah

Text © 2019 Luli Gray
Illustrations © 2019 Madelyn Goodnight

All rights reserved. Published 2019. Printed in Canada.

 This book is printed on paper certified to the environmental and social standards of the Forest Stewardship Council™ (FSC®).

Photo of Luli Gray: Photographer unknown
Photo of Madelyn Goodnight: Mary Kathryn Goodnight
Design: Shanna Compton

23 22 21 20 19   1 2 3 4 5
ISBN-13: 978-0-9996584-6-8 (hardcover)

Small press. Big conversations.
www.pennycandybooks.com

Old Esperanza's tree bore the sweetest pears in Spain, until a hailstorm froze every one. Esperanza wept, for without pears to sell, she would starve.

That night a poor woman knocked on her door.

"Please, I am *so* hungry," she said.

Although the larder held only one preserved pear, Esperanza served it to the beggar in her best bowl.

She gave up her own bed and slept on a chair.

Next morning Esperanza found her tree full of pears, the best crop ever.

All summer her nephew, Pablo, picked pears for market. Esperanza grew plump as the pears themselves.

The sweet fruit tempted the village children into the tree, where Esperanza found them sticky with juice, giggling at her.

"Stay there then," she said.

    The children grew sick of pears, but when they tried to climb down they stuck fast.

    "Help!" they cried. "We're stuck."

    "Nonsense," said Esperanza. "Come down at once."

    Instantly unstuck, they scampered home.

So everyone knew Esperanza could entrap anyone who climbed her tree.

One September day a smiling stranger stopped by her gate.

"Good day, Señor," said Esperanza.

"Good day, Esperanza," he said.

"How do you know my name? I don't know you."

"Forgive me, Señora," he said. "I mean no disrespect. But I know *you*, though we've never met till now. I've come for you."

Then she knew. Señor Death is sad when he takes a young person, full of possibilities, but for the old, he smiles, for he brings peace.

Peace! thought Esperanza. *Peace is for the dead.*

"Why didn't you come when I was weak and weary?" she cried. "Why now, when I am strong and happy?"

"I come when it's time," he said.

Esperanza's anger made even Death nervous, so he didn't notice her sly look.

"All right," she sighed. "Oh, to taste just one last pear . . . but I cannot climb."

"I can," said Death, and he swung himself up as Esperanza grinned like a cat full of stolen cream.

"I have it," said Señor Death, "a perfect pear, sweet as love." He started down.

"I'm stuck!" he cried. "I *must* come down, I have business in the next village, and there's war in a far country."

"Better to stay up there then," said Esperanza, shrugging.

Next day, as Pablo picked pears, Señor Death cried out for help, but Pablo was too young and strong to hear.

From then on, *nothing died*. People said it was a miracle.

In the war, Corporal Fox didn't die when Major Picaro chopped off his head. So the major put the corporal's head in his knapsack, slung the body over his saddle, and rode back to camp. There he laid the divided corporal on a cot and cared for him tenderly as a mother.

Soldiers sat around the battlefield, jeering at generals.

"Go soak your head, you military micklemuck," said a private, handing his enemy a sandwich. Thus the war ended.

Butcher shops closed because animals squawked, squealed, and mooed *after* they were cut up.

Could this be more curse than miracle?

"This must stop," said Señor Death.

"No," said Esperanza, "I refuse to die."

"You're a stubborn, wicked old woman," said Death.

"Stubborn, yes, as women must be, but wicked I'm not," retorted Esperanza.

"People are suffering!" Death shouted, pounding his branch.

"Suffering? Hah! You bring death to soldiers, to babies, to young girls."

"Esperanza," said Death, "I'm a servant of Fate, bringing sorrow or peace. It's not my choice."

"Then it's mine," said Esperanza. "I choose to live."

"There's a man in the next village," said Death. "Mortally ill, in great pain, longing for death."

"Why tell me?" Esperanza said.

"He is Miguel Alonzo," said Señor Death.

"My old friend?" cried Esperanza. "A stout man with a laughing wife named Anna?"

"He's no longer stout, nor has Anna laughed in many weeks," said Death.

Esperanza burst into tears.

"Truly," she sobbed, "life is as sweet to me as pears in honey, but I'll go if you bring Miguel peace. Come down, Señor."

With a loud pop like a cork coming out of a bottle, Señor Death's bony behind came unstuck, and down he scrambled.

"You're a good, strong-minded woman, quite rightly, I suppose," he said. "Because you've outwitted me, yet would give your life for Miguel's sake, you shall live as long as you like."

Death paused by the gate, watching Esperanza jig for joy.

"Remember," he said, "when you grow tired, call for me."

Esperanza gave a shockingly high kick for one so ancient.

"Don't hold your breath, old man!" she said, and went in to supper.

So, my dove, *that* is why there is always Death in the world, and why there is always Esperanza. For as you must surely know, in the language of Spain, Esperanza means Hope.

On the Origins of This Story

The Pear Tree is Luli Gray's retelling of an old folk tale called "Tia Miseria y la Muerte." The original tale is about an elderly woman whose tricking of death has serious unintended consequences for the world, but Luli makes some significant changes. It's not unusual to rework folktales (and certainly not unusual for Luli, who previously reworked Aesop's "The Ant and the Grasshopper" to be more hopeful), and versions of this one can be found in Puerto Rico, Spain, Portugal, and Brazil. A similar story known as "The Enchanted Apple Tree" comes from France and Flanders.

In these stories the old woman, known as Tia Miseria or Tante Misere (Aunt Misery), resists Death when he comes for her by causing him to get stuck in her magical tree. Trapped there, Death can no longer do his job. No one, not even the sick and afflicted and injured, can die. Whereas people suffered before, now their suffering is extended indefinitely, no end in sight. Finally Death begs her to free him so that he can make things right, but Tia Miseria only agrees if Death promises never to come for her again. Death agrees, and that's why, the stories conclude, misery still exists in the world.

The mean old woman is somewhat of a trope in fairy tales past and present. Think the wicked stepmother who tries to kill her stepdaughter; the witch who tries to cook the kids; Medusa; Baba Yaga; Cruella de Vil. But Tia Miseria's villainy just might outdo these villains: her selfishness explains why we all suffer.

But Tia Miseria doesn't appear in *The Pear Tree*. In Luli's telling, Tia Miseria's name is Esperanza, which is Spanish for *hope*, and instead of being the villain whose selfishness deepens suffering, Esperanza's compassion is ignited when she realizes that people are suffering because of her. In Luli's version "Miseria" is nowhere to be found. It's Esperanza who tricks Death, and it's Esperanza who sets him free to do his job and thus bring peace and calm to those who suffer. In other words, hope makes her want to live and, ultimately, hope compels her do the right thing. Luli's Esperanza is a complex character, more fully human than characters one typically sees in fairy tales in that she's a mix of good and bad instead of all one or the other.

Luli was ill when she wrote this story, and she died before we accepted it for publication. It feels fitting that the final story by such an accomplished writer would appear posthumously and be about a woman tricking death into granting her immortality. In a way, Luli has indeed become immortal. Her words live on and give us hope.

Penny Candy Books
October 2019

Luisa "Luli" Gray (1945–2017) was born in Buenos Aires, Argentina. She grew up in a bilingual family of readers, writers, and talkers, and though she always considered herself a writer—of mostly letters and comic verse—she did not begin writing fiction until 1987. After leaving her husband in 1971, she wandered all over Europe and Latin America, working as a barmaid, housemaid, short order cook, actress, singer, waitress, restaurant chef, and caterer before falling into food writing, more or less by accident. As an adult Luli lived in Boston and Greenwich Village for many years before moving to Chapel Hill, North Carolina, where she lived the rest of her life. Luli once said, "I write because it makes me happy, and I cannot think of a better way to make a living than by doing something I so dearly love." Her first novel, *Falcon's Egg*, was an ALA Notable Book.

Madelyn Goodnight knew during her time at the Rhode Island School of Design that she wanted to illustrate for kids. Growing up in Oklahoma gave her plenty of room to imagine, play, and dream about all the things she would experience when she grew up. Her family encouraged her to explore anything and everything, and shared a deep connection to their Native American heritage that emphasized the magic of storytelling. With each new book or piece of art that she makes, she's always trying to convey that magic. Madie uses a wide range of media and outlets for her art so that it is as diverse, energetic, and playful as the children who are seeing it.